CLOSER TO THE SUN

Written by Goddess Nefertari Illustrated by Tatenda Ndove

A story of affirmations used while on a journey through nature where a little girl gains her superpower that is enhanced by the sun.

BFF Publishing House is a Limited Liability Corporation dedicated wholly to the appreciation and publication of children and adults for the advancement of diversification in literature.

For more information on publishing contact

Antionette Mutcherson at
bff@bffpublishinghouse.com
Website: bffpublishinghouse.com
Published in the United States by
BFF Publishing House
Tallahassee, Florida First Edition, 2020

This book is dedicated to my beautiful loving mother, Phyllis Murray, who always supports my endeavors. Additionally, I dedicate this book to my family, friends, mentors and all my loved ones who have been so helpful, encouraging and supportive in my life. Last but not least, this book is also dedicated to all of my beautiful children in the world including my nieces and nephews. I want all of my children to know that you can fly in your power, do and be anything that you aspire to be. You are beautiful. It is important to learn balance and how to use positive affirmations to affirm your greatness.

- Goddess Nefertari

Today is a beautiful day!

I am grateful to breathe fresh air

I am grateful to be alive and well

I am going to use the power of my imagination to focus, relax, and just be me

I love you from my heart to yours!

As I fly in the sky,

I feel good

In the sky, I see

A group of heart-shaped butterflies nearby!

I slow down to feel their energy while breathing deeply

Take a deep breath in for five seconds, then breathe out....

Now, say,

"I am a beautiful butterfly

I can fly as far as a butterfly

I am free to spread my wings and fly wherever I want to go!"

As I fly in the sky,

I feel good

In the sky, I see

A white seagull nearby!

I stop to watch, and feel the seagull's energy while breathing deeply

Take a deep breath in for four seconds, then breathe out....

Now, say,

"I am as pure as a white seagull

I am as free as a bird

My wings fly high in the deep red and blue sky!"

As I sit still

Underneath the dragon blood tree,

I feel good

Suddenly, I see a dragonfly nearby!

I stop to watch and feel the dragonfly's energy while breathing deeply

Take a deep breath in for one second, then breathe out...

Now, say,

"I am peace

I am peaceful

Peace lives inside of me!"

As I fly in the sky,

I feel good

In the sky, I see

A red cardinal bird nearby!

I slow down to watch and feel the bird's energy while breathing deeply

Take a deep breath in for three seconds, then breathe out...

Now, say,

"I am gentle

I flow gently in the air

I am as beautiful as a red cardinal bird!"

As I sit still

Underneath the tree of life,

I feel good

In the air, I see

A colorful hummingbird nearby!

I stop to feel the hummingbird's energy while breathing deeply

Take a deep breath in for two seconds, then breathe out…

Now, say,

"I am love

I am loving

I can sing joyful, loving, and harmonious tunes like a hummingbird!"

I slowly open my eyes to a beautiful surprise!

A marula tree magically appears behind me, and a colorful ladybug too!

I stop to feel the ladybug's energy while breathing deeply

Take a deep breath in for five seconds, then breathe out…

Now, say,

"I am lucky every day and in every way

Good luck constantly flows in my life

I am as colorful and lively as a ladybug!"

As I lay in the green grass,

I feel good

Suddenly, the ground starts to shake—

Oh my!

An elephant is nearby!

I fly onto the elephant's back and a portal opened up for us to travel through

I fly along while breathing deeply

Take a deep breath in for four seconds, then breathe out...

"Now, say,

"I am powerful

I am a strong leader

I was born great

I was born to create, and use my brain power to its highest potential!"

As I rise above the green grass filled with sunflowers,

I feel good

I look up to see

The sun shining down on me!

Suddenly, I feel a light sensation in the middle of my forehead

My spirit sun is vibrating!

Now, I have the power to see, feel, and hear energy from my spirit sun in the middle of my forehead!

My heart and soul is free to fully express itself with love, inside out!

Take a deep breath in for three seconds, then breathe out...

As I stand in the green grass,

I feel good

Then, I suddenly feel a light sensation in the middle of my forehead!

I look up at the sunlight

The sun's ray flash down a big wooden drum

I close my eyes and play the drum while dancing

I can feel the energy from the drum throughout my entire body,

From the top of my head to the bottom of my feet!

Now, say,

"I am creative

Creativity lives within me

I am free to express my creativity!"

While sitting inside the blue lotus flower,

I feel another sensation on my forehead

I close my eyes to listen and feel the sun's energy while breathing deeply

Take a deep breath in for two seconds, then breathe out...

The sun shone down and brought me a beautiful mirror!

Now, say,

"I am the most unique soul in this world

I have the most unique magical powers that anyone has ever seen

I am naturally beautiful just the way I am

I am a shining, creative, energetic golden star!"

I love the sun because it gives me energy, vitamin D and enhances my brainpower.

CREATE YOUR OWN AFFIRMATIONS BELOW:

Example: I am love. I am a loving soul.

_____

_____

_____

_____

_____

_____

_____

_____

_____

_____

Shahgraphy

I am a beautiful soul with infinite potential. My name is Goddess Nefertari and I was born in Augusta, Ga. I am a creator with many gifts and talents. I love to teach, make crafts, jewelry, teach yoga, and spiritual empowerment. I love to love and express my creativity. I enjoy helping others especially the youth because they are our future leaders.

I share my gifts and knowledge with the community in many ways. I love my culture and expressing it to the world through creativity and art. I use my gifts to give back to the community and so much more. My love extends through the earth and the entire world. My motto is, "Do what you love and be free to be your authentic self!" Her story is greatness.

Made in the USA
Columbia, SC
04 August 2020